Noni Is Nervous

Heather Hartt-Sussman

Illustrated by
Geneviève Côté

TUNDRA BOOKS

Published in Canada by Tundra Books, a division of Random House of Canada Limited,
One Toronto Street, Suite 300, Toronto, Ontario M5C 2V6

Published in the United States by Tundra Books of Northern New York,
P.O. Box 1030, Plattsburgh, New York 12901

Library of Congress Control Number: 2012934218

Library and Archives Canada Cataloguing in Publication

Hartt-Sussman, Heather
     Noni is nervous / Heather Hartt-Sussman ; illustrated by
Geneviève Côté.

ISBN 978-1-77049-323-0. – ISBN 978-1-77049-395-7 (EPUB)

     I. Côté, Geneviève, 1964- II. Title.

PS8615.A757N65 2013   jC813'.6   C2012-901558-X

We acknowledge the financial support of the Government of Canada through the Canada Book
Fund and that of the Government of Ontario through the Ontario Media Development Corpora-
tion's Ontario Book Initiative. We further acknowledge the support of the Canada Council for the
Arts and the Ontario Arts Council for our publishing program.

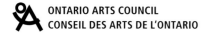

Edited by Sue Tate
Designed by Leah Springate
Medium: digital

www.tundrabooks.com

Printed and bound in Hong Kong

1 2 3 4 5 6   18 17 16 15 14 13

For my sons, Scotty and Jack,
and for my godson, Rod.

– H.H.S.

For teachers everywhere who are dedicated to making
their school a safe and happy place for every child.

– G.C.

Noni is nervous about a lot of things.
She is nervous about her playdates
with her bossy friend Susie.

She is nervous about global warming.

And, today, she is nervous about her first day of school.

Noni bites her nails.
   Noni twirls her hair.
   And she talks nonstop to calm her nerves.

   Her mama tells her to take her fingers out of her mouth.
   Her papa tells her to get her hands out of her hair.
   And her little brother tells her to stop going on and on about nothing.

When Noni was younger, there wasn't much to be nervous about. Except maybe a thunderstorm.

And strange dogs.

And monsters under the bed.

Mostly she stayed by her mama's side, and all was well with the world.

But now she has to go to school,
and Noni is a nervous wreck!
What will she wear?
Where will she sit?

What if the teacher is mean?

When the bus pulls up, Noni is nervous.
In the school yard, Noni is nervous.

When she meets her teacher, Noni
is still nervous.

Noni bites her nails.
Noni twirls her hair.
And she talks to her neighbor long after
the teacher asks the class to settle down.

When Noni gets home, her mama asks her what she learned.

Her papa asks her <u>whom</u> she met.

And her little brother asks her where she sat.

But Noni was so nervous, she forgot to remember a thing!

That night, her mama tells her to try and make a friend.

Her papa says feeling comfortable at school takes practice, practice, practice.

And her brother names all the friends he's made at *Mommy and Me*.

The next day, when she gets on the bus, Noni sits beside a girl from her class.

"I'm Noni," she says nervously.

"I'm Briar," says the girl.

Briar is what Mama calls outgoing. And before you know it, she is introducing Noni to Abigail and Kasey, Xavier and Brooke.

That wasn't so bad, thinks Noni, though she is still nervous about getting lost at school.

She's nervous about opening her juice box by herself.

And Noni is very nervous about having an accident!

Noni bites her nails.
Noni twirls her hair.
And she talks nonstop to Briar, even though she has nothing in particular to say.

At school, Noni has a fine time.
    She doesn't get lost.
    She doesn't have any trouble opening her juice box.
    And Noni doesn't have one single accident.

When Noni gets home, her mama rings her hands and asks, "How was school?"

Her papa paces and asks, "Did you make a friend?"

Her brother just shakes his head. Knowing Noni, her chances don't look good.

Her mama bites her nails.
Her papa twirls his hair.
And her brother talks nonstop
about nonsense, like dinosaur
bones and alien abductions.

But Noni clears her throat and announces: "School was great! *Sheesh!* I really don't know what you are all so nervous about!"